Jane as Narrator . . . . Naia Kelly

Kerchak . . . . Lance Henriksen

Kala . . . . Glenn Close

Terk . . . . Rosie O'Donnell

Tantor . . . . Wayne Knight

Jane . . . . Minnie Driver

Tarzan . . . . Tony Goldwyn

Professor Porter . . . . Nigel Hawthorne

Clayton . . . . Brian Blessed

Read & Sing Along produced by Randy Thornton and Ted Kryczko
Adapted by Wendy Vinitsky
Engineered by Jeff Sheridan
Art Direction by Luis M. Fernández
Design by Marcella Wong and Tiffany Quon
Illustrations by The Walt Disney Studios

Based on the animated film Disney's *Tarzan*®
Produced by Bonnie Arnold
Directed by Kevin Lima and Chris Buck
Screenplay by Tab Murphy and Bob Tzudiker & Noni White
Songs by Phil Collins
Original Score by Mark Mancina

WALT DISNEY
R E C O R D S
Burbank, CA 91521
Printed in U.S.A.

DISNEY'S
TARZAN
READ & SING ALONG

WALT DISNEY RECORDS

Hello. My name is Jane, and I'd like to tell you the story of Tarzan. You can follow along with me in your book. When you hear this sound . . . it's time to turn the page. Are you ready? Let's begin.

It all started when Daddy and I went to Africa to study gorillas – a lifelong dream of his, really. So there I was, dressed for a stroll in Kensington Gardens, but crawling through the jungle with Daddy and Clayton, the fellow we'd hired to be our guide. Clayton kept firing his gun into the air, undoubtedly scaring away any gorillas. The next thing I knew, I was swinging through the trees in the clutches of a wild man! But I'm afraid I'm getting a bit ahead of myself, so I'll slow down and start at the very beginning.

Tarzan was just a baby when Kala found him in a tree house in the jungle. Kala was a mother gorilla who had lost her own baby to Sabor the leopard – the same leopard who had killed Tarzan's parents. Kala took Tarzan home to care for him. But Kerchak, the leader of the gorilla family, thought that Tarzan's presence was a threat to the gorillas.

"Kala, I cannot let you put our
family in danger."
"Does he look dangerous to you?"
"Was it alone?"
"Yes. There are no others."
"Then you may keep him."
"Kerchak, I know
he'll be a good son."
"I said he could stay.
That doesn't make
him my son!"

You'll Be in My Heart

Come, stop your crying
It'll be all right
Just take my hand, hold it tight
I will protect you from all around you
I will be here, don't you cry

For one so small, you seem so strong
My arms will hold you
Keep you safe and warm
This bond between us can't be broken

I will be here, don't you cry

'Cause you'll be in my heart
Yes, you'll be in my heart
from this day on
now and forever more
You'll be in my heart
no matter what they say
You'll be here in my heart always
Always

Music and Lyrics by Phil Collins
Performed by Phil Collins and Glenn Close
Produced by Phil Collins and Mark Mancina
COPYRIGHT © 1999 Edgar Rice Burroughs, Inc. and
Walt Disney Music Company (ASCAP). All Rights Reserved.
℗ 1999 Edgar Rice Burroughs, Inc. and Walt Disney Records.

As Tarzan grew up with the gorillas, he made friends with Terk and Tantor, an elephant who couldn't quite figure Tarzan out.

"Ya know, I've been thinking lately that maybe Tarzan could be some subspecies of elephant."

"What – are you crazy? An elephant?"

"Listen to me, think about it. He enjoys a peanut. I enjoy a peanut."

"He looks nothing like you!"

But even though Tarzan didn't look like anyone else in the jungle, he thrived because he was a keen observer and could imitate anything that moved. Tarzan was able to swing through the trees like a monkey and was as at home in the water as a hippo. But no matter what Tarzan did, Kerchak wouldn't accept him.

Then one day Sabor, the leopard, paid another visit to the gorilla family. Kerchak tried to protect his clan, but he nearly lost his life doing so – until Tarzan came to his aid.

When Tarzan lifted Sabor's lifeless body over his head, the gorillas cheered. Their worst enemy had been defeated. All the apes rushed over to Tarzan to congratulate him, but he was concerned about Kerchak. Out of respect for the ape leader, he laid Sabor at his feet and bowed before him.

It was about this time that Daddy and I arrived in Africa. As we searched for gorillas, Clayton, our guide, kept firing his gun. It was a strange sound to Tarzan and the other creatures.

"What was that?"

Kerchak gave the orders. "Everyone, let's move." But Tarzan was curious, so he searched for the cause of the unfamiliar sound. And that's when he saw us – his first human beings.

Suddenly a papaya fell out of a tree and clunked me on the head. Then the cutest little baby baboon came running after it. I reached for my sketchbook and quickly started drawing the little fellow. But before I could finish, he snatched the book and took off.

I chased after him and found myself face-to-face
with the rest of his family. They were angry with me for
upsetting the youngster, so they chased *me*! And that's
how I ended up swinging through the trees with Tarzan.
He saved me from the baboons. It was terribly romantic –
except I didn't think so at the time!

   "Oh! Oh! I'm f-flying! What on earth am I – ? Let go of
me! Ow! Aaaah!"

I didn't know which was more frightening: boiling-mad baboons chewing on my boots or jungle acrobatics with an ape man! Finally we landed in a tree, and that's when he started examining my feet, my face . . .

"Don't come any closer. Please don't!"

. . . and he listened to my heart . . . and brought my head close to listen to his heart . . .

"Yes, thank you. It's a lovely heartbeat. It's very nice."

Then he repeated my words! "It's very nice."

"You *do* speak! And all this time I thought you were just a big, wild, quiet, silent person . . . thing. Why didn't you tell me? I mean, I must say, I'm rather curious as to who you are. I mean, I'd love to – "

"Tarzan."

"Tar-zan. Oh, I see. I'm Jane."

"I'm Jane."

"No, no." I pointed at him. "Tarzan." Then I pointed to myself. "Jane."

"Jane."

"Extraordinary. Um, please, can you take me to my camp?" And off we went, sailing through the trees again.

As we got closer and closer to camp, we could hear
some kind of racket going on. It turned out to be gorillas,
and they'd made a mess of our things! But what was even
more surprising was that the gorillas
were happy to see Tarzan.
"He's one of them!" I stood
watching in amazement.

Suddenly I felt hot breath on the back of my neck. When I turned around, the biggest gorilla I'd ever seen was staring down at me.

"Oh, my!" Then I heard Daddy.

"Jane! Jane! Where are you, Jane?"

The big gorilla motioned for the others to follow him, which they did, but Tarzan acted as if he wanted to stay. Just as Daddy and Clayton hurried into camp, he slipped away.

"Oh, Jane! Oh, thank goodness!"

"Good heavens! What happened?"

When Tarzan and the gorillas were safely home again, Kerchak gave firm orders. "Everyone, we will avoid the strangers. Do not let them see you and do not seek them out."

"They mean us no harm, Kerchak!"

"Tarzan, I don't know that."

"But I do. I've spent time with them."

"You may be willing to risk our safety, but I'm not."

"Why are you threatened by anyone different from you?"

"Protect this family and stay away from them."

Tarzan turned to his mother. "Why didn't you tell me there were creatures that look like me?"

Back at camp I tried describing Tarzan, but Clayton thought I had lost my mind!

"Professor, you are here to find gorillas! Not indulge some girlish fantasy."

"Fantasy! I didn't imagine him. Tarzan is . . . real." And proving my argument, Tarzan dropped out of the trees into our camp.

Daddy became excited. "It's him-h-it's h-him-TARZAN!"

Clayton grabbed for his gun. "Professor! Jane! Stand back!"

But I got in between him and Tarzan. "Mr. Clayton. I think I'll take it from here." And that's when I began to introduce Tarzan to the rest of the world – through books and pictures, of course – and Tarzan showed me the wonders of his jungle home.

Strangers Like Me

Whatever you do, I'll do it too
Show me everything and tell me how
It all means something, and yet nothing to me
I can see there's so much to learn
It's all so close and yet so far
I see myself as people see me
Oh, I just know there's something bigger out there

Chorus:
I wanna know
Can you show me?
I wanna know about these strangers like me
Tell me more
Please show me
Something's familiar about these strangers like me

Every gesture, every move that she makes
Makes me feel like never before
Why do I have this growing need to be beside her?
Ooo, these emotions I never knew
Of some other world far beyond this place
Beyond the trees, above the clouds
I see before me a new horizon

Chorus

Come with me now to see my world
Where there's beauty beyond your dreams
Can you feel the things I feel right now with you?
Take my hand, there's a world I need to know

Chorus
. . . I wanna know

Music and Lyrics by Phil Collins
Performed by Phil Collins
Produced by Phil Collins

As the days went by, Clayton grew more and more impatient with Tarzan's questions about the outside world.

"We've wasted all this time on what he wants. The boat could arrive any day. Now, ask him straight out."

So I began slowly. "Tarzan, will you take us to the gorillas?"

"I can't."

"Why not, Tarzan?"

"Kerchak." But we didn't know what "Kerchak" meant, so Clayton grabbed Tarzan's shoulder and shoved a picture of a gorilla in his face. Tarzan pushed past him and walked away.

The next time Tarzan visited our camp, we were
being forced to pack up. "Tarzan! Oh, I was so afraid that
you wouldn't come in time. The boat's arrived. The boat
that's come to take us home, to England. And Daddy and I
were wond – well, I was wondering . . . well, we really
hope that you'll come with us. Won't you?"

    "Jane must stay with Tarzan."

       "Wha-? Stay here? Oh, d-d-don't . . ."

       "Please."

         Well, I hadn't even considered
staying. It was an outlandish idea!
But I also realized that I had become
fond of life in the jungle. I ran from
Tarzan so he wouldn't see my tears.

As soon as I was out of sight, Clayton hinted to Tarzan that if he led us to the gorillas, I would stay in Africa. So Terk and Tantor distracted Kerchak, and Tarzan took us to the gorilla nesting area. The first gorilla we saw was Kala.

"She's beautiful!"

"She's my mother."

"Th-this is your . . . mother?"

Tarzan tried coaxing her towards us, but Kala disappeared into the trees. The little ones weren't bashful. They climbed all over me, touching my hair. I imitated the sound that Tarzan was making. "Oo-oo-ee-eh-ou. Oo-oo-ee-eh-ou. Good heavens! What did I say?"

"That Jane stays with Tarzan."

"Stay? But I-I thought we'd already . . . Oh, Tarzan."

Suddenly Kerchak burst through the bushes and attacked Clayton. Tarzan had to wrestle him away so we could all escape. "Go! Now!"

Kerchak was shocked that Tarzan had defended us.

"Kerchak . . . I didn't . . . I'm sorry . . . I–"

"I asked you to protect our family. And you betrayed us all."

That evening, Kala took Tarzan to the tree house. In the dusty, vine-covered room, Tarzan found a picture of himself with his parents.

"Is this me? And this is my father? And, and my . . ."

"Now you know. Tarzan, I just want you to be happy . . . whatever you decide."

"No matter where I go, you will always be my mother."

"And you will always be in my heart."

No sooner had we boarded the ship, than Clayton's men took us prisoner. Clayton sneered at Tarzan. "So sorry about the rude welcome, old boy, but I couldn't have you making a scene when we put your furry friends in their cages."

Tarzan was baffled. "Why?"

"Why? For three hundred pounds sterling a head! Actually I have you to thank, my boy. Couldn't have done it without you."

With his gun fully loaded, Clayton and his men headed back to shore in the launch.

Meanwhile, Terk and Tantor had raced to the beach, hoping to say good-bye to Tarzan. They were too late. The ship was far from shore. Suddenly they heard Tarzan's yell.

"That sounded like Tarzan! He sounded like, like he was in trouble."

The two friends began swimming out to sea. When they got to the ship, they managed to haul themselves onboard. From down in the hold, I thought the ship had hit something.

"What was that?"

"That sounded just like an elephant." Then Tantor's foot crashed through the ceiling, just missing Daddy's head.

"Tantor!" Tarzan pulled himself up on deck.
"Thanks, guys!"

Terk started to cry. "I thought I would never see
you again!"

Moments later, Clayton and his men charged into the
gorillas' home and forced the animals into cages. But
Clayton pointed his gun at Kerchak. "I think this one will
be better off stuffed."

All of a sudden Tarzan came swinging into camp and
knocked Clayton off his feet.

Kerchak was surprised. "You came back."

"I came home."

Then Clayton began shooting at Tarzan, but Kerchak charged at Clayton and got hit by a bullet. Kerchak fell. Clayton kept firing. So Tarzan lured Clayton into the jungle. When Tarzan took to the trees, Clayton climbed after him. But Tarzan dropped down onto him and grabbed his gun.

Clayton tried to act brave. "Go ahead. Shoot me. Be a man."

But Tarzan wouldn't be tricked into stupid behavior. "Not a man like you." He smashed Clayton's gun against the tree and tossed it away. Then he started climbing again. Clayton followed, so Tarzan used the tree's vines like lassos and whipped them expertly around Clayton's arms. Clayton slashed wildly at the vines, trying to free himself. Tarzan warned him, "Clayton, don't!" But Clayton ignored him, the vines broke, and Clayton fell to his death.

Kerchak was lying on the ground, taking his last breath, as Tarzan rushed to his side. "Kerchak, forgive me."

"No. Forgive me for not understanding . . . that you have always been one of us. Our family will look to you now."

"No, Kerchak . . ."

"Take care of them, my son."

The next morning, I said good-bye to Tarzan. "London will seem so small compared to all this."

"I will miss you, Jane . . . good-bye."

As we set sail, Daddy was sad too. "Good-bye, Tarzan! . . . Oh, I'm going to miss that boy . . . Jane, dear, I can't help feeling that you should stay."

"Daddy, please don't. We've been through all of this. I couldn't possibly . . . I belong in England with you, with people – "

In that instant a gust of wind took one of my gloves. As I tried to grab it, I saw it land at Tarzan's feet.

Gently, Daddy tried again. "But you love him. Go on."

Without a moment's thought, I jumped overboard, splashed my way to Tarzan, and kissed him. Then Daddy had a brilliant idea.

"Captain, tell them that you never found us, eh. After all, people get lost in the jungle every day, eh? Tootle pip!" And Daddy jumped overboard too.

On shore, the entire ape family welcomed us, and I answered them back. "Oo-oo-ee-eh-ou." We leaped on top of Tantor and headed for our new home.